Happy 2nd Birthday!

Happy Birthday!
Enjoy your special day!

You are turning **two** today,
it's such a special day!

You're going to have a party,
where the kids can play and play.

Your friends will come
to celebrate...

They'll have a lot of fun.

They'll play some games,

and have some cake,

and skip, and jump, and run!

You might have cotton candy...

and you might play on the slide!

Or maybe a nice puppet show,
if you all stay inside!

They'll bring balloons,
and presents...

And there might just be a clown!

And some of your good buddies
will be jumping up and down!

Maybe you will go outside,
and play with all your friends.

The day will be your special day,
from morning till it ends.

So, Happy, Happy Birthday!

To a boy who's really sweet!

A boy that's super-special...

from his head
down to his feet!

Happy Birthday

Happy 2nd Birthday!

Sally was born in Jackson, Michigan. She has lived all over the country with her husband, Fred. They have 3 grown children, and they all live in Louisville, KY. She has written over 30 children's books and had her first book published in 2000. Sneaky Snail Stories are all sweet and simple rhyming books with really cute illustrations. You can see all the Sneaky Snail Stories at: www.sneakysnailstories.com
Other books by Sally:

No Pancakes for Puppy
Grandma and Grandpa Love You
Your Aunt Loves You
The Best Day

Emma's Hilarious Horse Book (personalized for boys or girls with cats, dogs, penguins or frogs)
Emma, the Super, Amazing, Awesome, Intelligent, Girly-Girl (personalized)
Noah the Basketball Star (personalized for several sports for boys or girls)
Noah's Very Own Cook Book (personalized for boys or girls)
Grandma and Grandpa Love Emma (personalized from any relative for boys or girls)
Emma Turns One! (personalized for boys or girls ages 1-6)   and many more....

website: www.sneakysnailstories.com   facebook: Sneaky Snail Stories
Etsy: (search for) thesneakysnailstore   Amazon: (search for) Sally Helmick North

The Best Day!

written and illustrated by Sally Helmick North

No Cookies for Kitty!

written and illustrated by Sally Helmick North

No Pancakes for Puppy!

written and illustrated by Sally Helmick North

Grandma and Grandpa Love You!

written and illustrated by Sally Helmick North

Made in the USA
Middletown, DE
11 February 2017